Dear Parent:

Congratulations! Your child is taking the first steps on an exciting journey. The destination? Independent reading!

STEP INTO READING® will help your child get there. The program offers five steps to reading success. Each step includes fun stories and colorful art. There are also Step into Reading Sticker Books, Step into Reading Math Readers, Step into Reading Write-In Readers, Step into Reading Phonics Readers, and Step into Reading Phonics First Steps! Boxed Sets—a complete literacy program with something for every child.

Learning to Read, Step by Step!

Ready to Read Preschool–Kindergarten
• big type and easy words • rhyme and rhythm • picture clues
For children who know the alphabet and are eager to begin reading.

Reading with Help Preschool–Grade 1
• basic vocabulary • short sentences • simple stories
For children who recognize familiar words and sound out new words with help.

Reading on Your Own Grades 1–3
• engaging characters • easy-to-follow plots • popular topics
For children who are ready to read on their own.

Reading Paragraphs Grades 2–3
• challenging vocabulary • short paragraphs • exciting stories
For newly independent readers who read simple sentences with confidence.

Ready for Chapters Grades 2–4
• chapters • longer paragraphs • full-color art
For children who want to take the plunge into chapter books but still like colorful pictures.

STEP INTO READING® is designed to give every child a successful reading experience. The grade levels are only guides. Children can progress through the steps at their own speed, developing confidence in their reading, no matter what their grade.

Remember, a lifetime love of reading starts with a single step!

For Lilly Grace—M.L.

Step into Reading, Random House, and the Random House colophon are registered trademarks of Random House, Inc.

Visit us on the Web!
www.stepintoreading.com
www.randomhouse.com/kids

Educators and librarians, for a variety of teaching tools, visit us at
www.randomhouse.com/teachers

Library of Congress Cataloging-in-Publication Data
Lagonegro, Melissa.
A cars christmas / by Melissa Lagonegro. — 1st ed.
p. cm.
ISBN 978-0-7364-2611-4 (trade) — ISBN 978-0-7364-8071-0 (lib. bdg.)
I. Cars (Motion picture) II. Title. PZ7.L14317Car 2009 [E]—dc22 2008047468

Printed in the United States of America   20 19 18 17 16 15 14 13

DISNEY · PIXAR
THE WORLD OF
Cars

A CARS CHRISTMAS

By Melissa Lagonegro
Illustrated by the Disney Storybook Artists
Inspired by the art and character designs created by Pixar

Random House 🏠 New York

It is Christmastime in Radiator Springs!

4

Oh, what fun
the holiday brings!

Lightning and Sally
trim the tire tree.

Mater hangs
lights carefully.

Flo serves oilcans
tied with bows.

Red has ribbons
on his fire hose.

Sarge leads
the group ahead.

Mater pulls
a big red sled.

Ramone paints stripes
on Lightning McQueen.

He picks the colors
red and green.

Lizzie sells stickers
to holiday buyers.

Luigi makes wreaths
from ribbons and tires.

Cars drive home
after shopping all day.

Sheriff makes sure they
are stopping on the way.

Lightning dashes
through the snow.

Mater is ready
if he needs a tow.

Guido shines
every snow tire.

Sally warms up
over a fire.

Doc fills Sarge
with antifreeze.

Mistletoe makes

Mater sneeze.

Fillmore fills cars
with nice warm fuel.

Lightning goes to
snowplow school.

The town is filled
with holiday cheer.

Copperheads

ABDO
Publishing Company

A Buddy Book
by
Julie Murray

VISIT US AT
www.abdopub.com

Published by Buddy Books, an imprint of ABDO Publishing Company, 4940 Viking Drive, Suite 622, Edina, Minnesota 55435. Copyright © 2005 by Abdo Consulting Group, Inc. International copyrights reserved in all countries. No part of this book may be reproduced in any form without written permission from the publisher.

Printed in the United States.

Edited by: Christy DeVillier
Contributing Editors: Matt Ray, Michael P. Goecke
Graphic Design: Maria Hosley
Image Research: Deborah Coldiron
Photographs: Corel, Mark Kostich, Minden Pictures, Photodisc, Photospin

Library of Congress Cataloging-in-Publication Data

Murray, Julie, 1969-
  Copperheads/Julie Murray.
      p. cm. — (Animal kingdom. Set II)
  Includes bibliographical references (p.).
  Contents: Snakes — Copperheads — Size and color — Their bodies — Where they live — What they eat — Senses — Defenses — Babies.
  ISBN 1-59197-309-0
    1. Copperhead—Juvenile literature. [1. Copperhead. 2. Snakes.] I. Title.

QL666.O69 M873 2003
597.96'3—dc21

                                            2002038502

Contents

Snakes

Snakes have been around more than 100 million years. Today, there are more than 3,000 kinds of snakes. They live in many parts of the world.

Snakes are **reptiles**. Reptiles need outside heat to warm themselves. Without heat, reptiles become cold and slow moving. Snakes and other reptiles lie in sunshine to get warm. Lizards, crocodiles, alligators, and turtles are reptiles, too.

The world is full of many kinds of snakes.

5

Copperheads

Copperhead snakes have a copper-colored head. This is why they are called copperheads. Copper is the color of a penny.

There are five main kinds of copperheads:

1. broad-banded
2. northern
3. southern
4. Osage
5. trans-Pecos

Copperhead snakes are pit vipers. Pit vipers have **venom** and hollow **fangs**. Venom is a poison. It makes the pit viper's bite deadly.

A copperhead's fangs fold back when it is not using them.

What They Look Like

Copperheads grow to become about 30 inches (76 cm) long. They may be many shades of brown or gray. Some northern and southern copperheads have pink colors, too. Most copperheads have darker bands around their bodies. Young copperheads often have yellow or green tails.

A copperhead has two pits on its head. They lie between the nose and eyes. These pits help copperheads sense heat. They can sense heat from other animals. This helps copperheads and other pit vipers find **prey**.

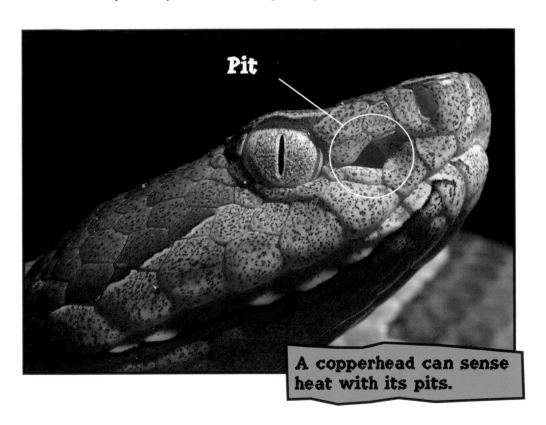

Pit

A copperhead can sense heat with its pits.

Special Skin

Copperheads and other snakes have skin made of scales. Scales are tiny, hard plates. They protect the snake's body. Other reptiles have scaly skin, too.

Snakes can grow new skin. When the new skin is ready, they will shed their old skin. This is called molting.

A snake's skin is made up of tiny scales.

10

Where They Live

Copperheads live only in North America. They live in southern and eastern parts of the United States.

Copperheads live on grasslands and rocky hillsides. They live near lakes and streams, too. Copperheads often hide under woodpiles or rocks.

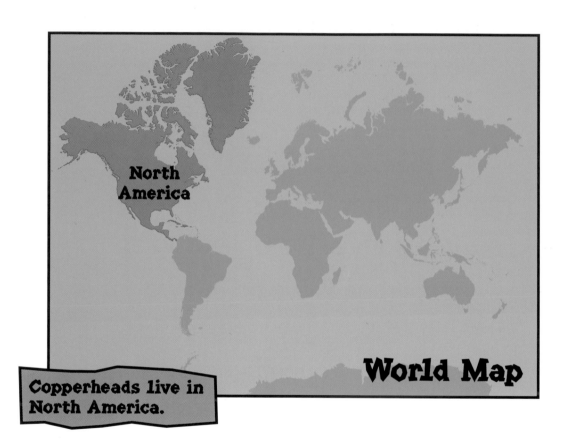

North
America

World Map

Copperheads live in
North America.

Copperheads **hibernate** in dens during the winter. A den is a hidden place. A copperhead's den may be a hole in the ground. Copperheads often share their dens with other hibernating snakes. They leave their dens in the spring.

A copperhead begins looking for a den in late fall.

Hunting And Eating

Like all snakes, copperheads only eat meat. They eat insects, mice, frogs, lizards, birds, and other snakes.

Copperheads eat mice and other small animals.

Copperheads use their special pits to find **prey**. They often look for food at night. They hide and catch prey by surprise. A copperhead's quick bite sends **venom** into the prey's body. The venom poisons and kills the animal.

Copperheads often hunt at night.

Snakes can stretch their mouths very wide to eat. They swallow their food whole. Many snakes can eat animals that are wider than them!

This egg-eater snake is swallowing a large egg.

Hiding helps copperheads catch prey by surprise.

Copperhead Babies

Female copperheads have their babies in August or September. As many as eight babies may be born at one time.

A baby copperhead grows inside its mother. It is born alive inside a soft egg. A newborn copperhead breaks out of its egg right away.

Newborn copperheads are between eight and ten inches (20 and 25 cm) long. They have **venom** and know how to hunt. Baby copperheads can take care of themselves.

Copperheads can live as long as 25 years in the wild.

Helpful Snakes

Some people think copperheads are good for nothing. This is not true. Copperheads eat pests, such as mice and rats.

Rats are pests for many people.

A copperhead's **venom** can be helpful, too. People can turn snake venom into **antivenin**. Antivenin helps people recover from snakebites. People hope to make other helpful medicines from venom. One day, venom may help people recover from deadly illnesses.

People "milk" snakes for their helpful venom.

Important Words

antivenin a medicine that helps people recover from snakebites.

fang a long, narrow tooth.

hibernate to spend the winter sleeping.

molt to shed and grow new skin.

prey an animal that is food for other animals.

reptiles scaly-skinned animals that cannot make heat inside their bodies.

venom the harmful poison made by copperheads and other animals.

Web Sites

To learn more about copperheads, visit ABDO Publishing Company on the World Wide Web. Web sites about copperheads are featured on our Book Links page. These links are routinely monitored and updated to provide the most current information available.

www.abdopub.com

Index